For Jane

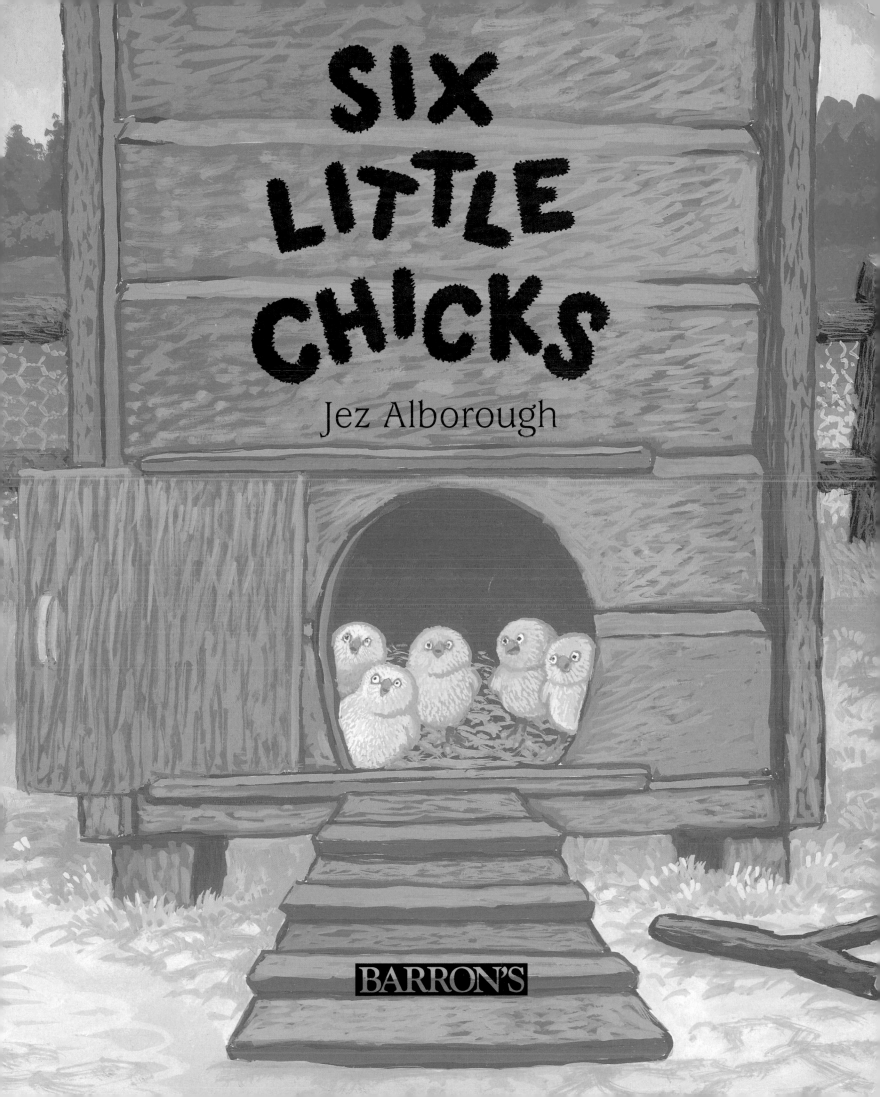

The sun looked down on a beautiful day
and five little chicks came out to play,

but Hen stepped back in the old chicken hut

and sat on her egg, with both eyes shut.

Then came Owl with a **SWOOP SWOOP SWOOP**
as he flapped around the back of the chicken coop.
"TO-WIT TO-WOO, watch out!" cried Owl.
"The big bad fox is on the prowl."

"The fox!" clucked Hen. "I must check on my chicks."
She ran through the straw with a **CLICK CLACK CLICK**

then stuck out her head through the chicken hut door,
and there in the chicken coop this is what she saw . . .

The first little
chick going

PECK
PECK
PECK

The second little
chick going

CHEEP
CHEEP
CHEEP

The third little
chick going

FLAP FLAP
FLAP

And the fifth little chick
playing with a stick,
lying on his back going

KICK
KICK
KICK

The fourth little
chick going

HOP HOP
HOP

Hen looked right,

Hen looked left,

Hen looked in between,

but the hairy, scary big bad fox was nowhere to be seen.

She told her chicks, "Play close to the door,"

then went to sit on the egg once more.

Next came Goose with a **STRUT STRUT STRUT**
to the crack at the back of the old chicken hut.
"HONK HONK HONK! Watch out!" cried Goose.
"The big bad fox is on the loose."

"The big bad fox!" clucked Hen. "Are you sure?
I had a good look and he wasn't there before."

She **CLICK CLACK CLICKED** to the chicken hut door,
and there in the chicken coop this is what she saw . . .

Hen looked left, Hen looked right, Hen looked all around,
but the hairy, scary big bad fox was nowhere to be found.

"Play closer to the door," clucked Hen,

and she sat down to wait on her egg **AND THEN** . . .

"WATCH OUT, WATCH OUT!" a scary voice cried. "THE BIG BAD FOX IS RIGHT OUTSIDE!"

"That does it!" clucked Hen—
she ran through the straw
and called to her chicks
from the chicken hut door.

"Five little chicks—
now do as I say,
playtime is over,
come in right away."

They ran up the ramp
with a **CLICK CLACK CLICK.**
"Hurry!" clucked Hen.
"Be **QUICK QUICK QUICK!**

Now stay in the hut,
and don't make a sound,
just wait while I go
for a good look around."

"I CAN SMELL CHICKS," said a voice. "HELL-O!"

Who was it? The five little chicks didn't know.

"**COME CLOSER,**" said the voice, "**JUST A BIT MORE.**"

So the chicks stepped closer,

and then they saw . . .

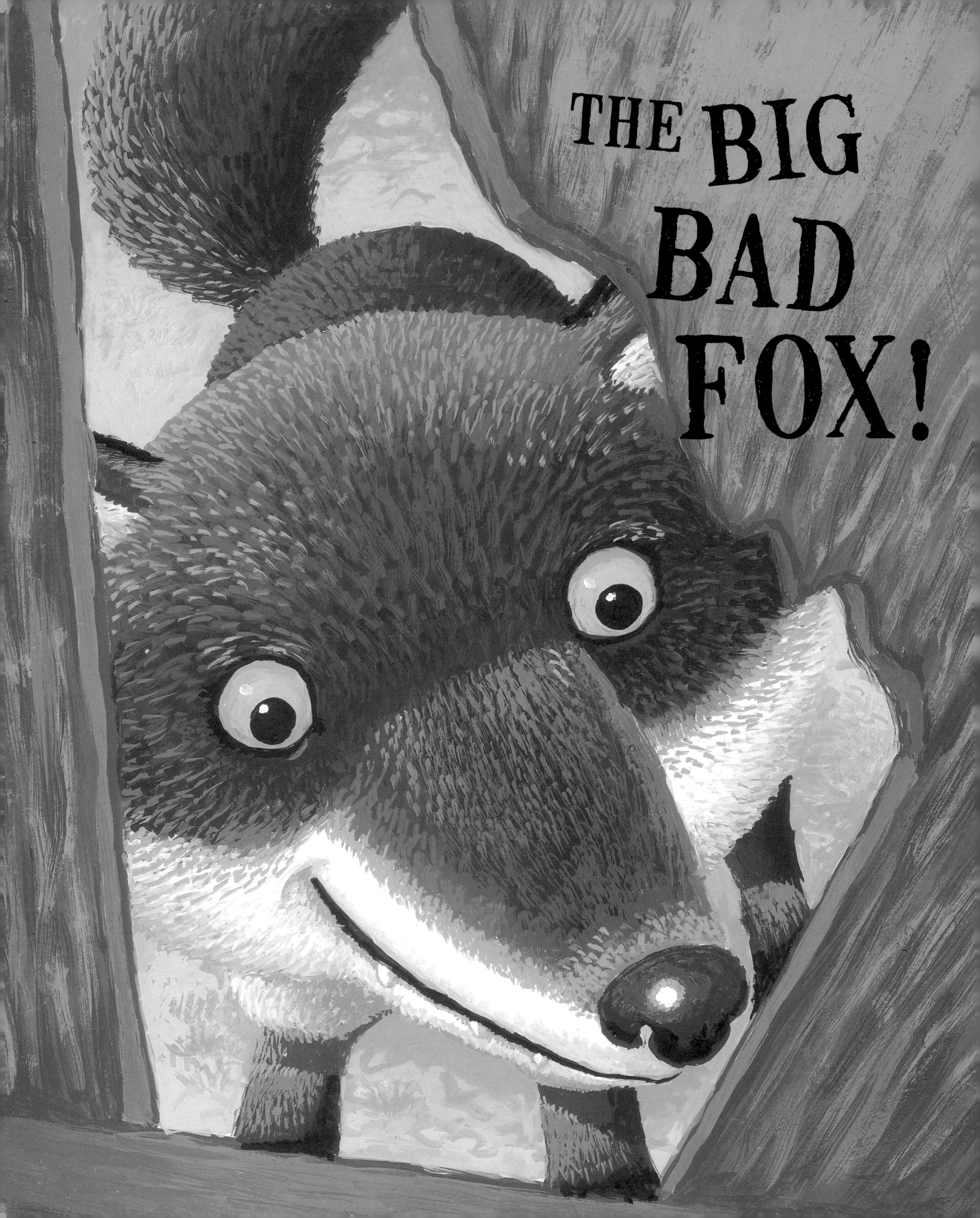
THE BIG
BAD
FOX!

He sniffed through the crack and he tried to squeeze in,
with his long pointy snout and his big toothy grin.

He pushed and he shoved then he pushed a bit more
until his head was inside and then he saw . . .

The first little chick going
PECK
PECK
PECK

The second little chick going
CHEEP
CHEEP
CHEEP

The third little chick going
FLAP FLAP
FLAP

The fourth little chick going

HOP

HOP

HOP

"

"

And lying on his back, the fifth little chick gave his stick

a great

big

KICK!

The fox licked his lips, "HEE HEE HEE!
FIVE LITTLE CHICKS, YOU CAN'T HURT ME!
I'LL TAKE MY PICK, YOU'RE CAUGHT IN A TRAP!"
Then he opened his jaws and went SNAP SNAP

Four little chicks went
RUN RUN RUN,
as over their heads the
kicked stick spun.

SNAP

The big bad fox was out of luck . . .
now his jaws were **STUCK STUCK STUCK!**

"The fox!" cried Owl with a **SWOOP SWOOP SWOOP**.

"The fox is in the chicken coop!"

"Quick!" yelled Goose with a **STRUT STRUT STRUT**.

"His head's inside the chicken hut!"

SCRATCH
SCRATCH
SCRATCH

The big bad fox had met his match.

With a **CLICK CLACK CLICK** then came Hen,

now they were all together again.

She cuddled and counted her five little chicks . . .

the egg went CRACK and then there were . . . .